Christmas Crackers for Cats
Festive Feline Limericks

Julie and John Hope

www.cato9tales.com

Contents

Chapter 1: Misfortune

There is an old cat from Duluth
With one eye and hardly a tooth
Eats food with a paw
Drinks milk through a straw
Which makes her look rather uncouth

❊ ❊ ❊

A cat whose depression was chronic
Who blamed it on being Slavonic
Invented a draught
That made everyone laugh
And patented is as Cat-a-Tonic

❄ ❄ ❄

A vain Siamese who's called Peter
Was sitting too close to the heater
His tail it did smoke
But he made it a joke
Insisting his rear would look neater

❄ ❄ ❄

Chapter 2: Travel

A wandering kitty called Romulus
Caught buses to add to his stimulus
They said he was fey
Never losing his way
And always got off at the terminus

(A cautionary tail!)

❋ ❋ ❋

A holiday junkie called Grace
Would hide in her human's suitcase
And off she would fly
To Spain or Shanghai
It really was worth the disgrace

❋ ❋ ❋

Chapter 3: The Snip

A raunchy old tomcat called Bertie
Had a mind that was ever so dirty
Now his goolies have gone
He's just one peeping Tom
So all he can do is get flirty

❄ ❄ ❄

I'm a naughty old tomcat called Ming
Twice weekly I go on a fling
I'm so often smitten
I lose count of my kittens
Perhaps they should tie up my thing!

❄ ❄ ❄

Chapter 4: Arts, Culture and Media

A musical cat Salome
Would listen to opera all day
And with her hind feet
She'd tap out the beat
To Verdi, Mozart and Bizet

❄ ❄ ❄

A moggy who owned a TV
Would only watch Wildlife on Three
And you haven't a hope
Of watching a soap
For he hides the remote up a tree

❄ ❄ ❄

A theatrical kitty called Saul
Not wanting to hear a catcall
Got his friends from the press
The performance to bless
Now it's encores and fine caterwaul

❄ ❄ ❄

A cultural kitty called Strauss
Would visit the Grand Opera House
And wouldn't you know
His favourite show
Was the wonderful Die Fledermaus

❄ ❄ ❄

A cat prodigy called Louise
Could play the piano with ease
Now she could be a star
But won't go too far
As she really can't reach all the keys

❄ ❄ ❄

Chapter 5: Toilet

A dirty old cat from Bilox
Would not let you clean out his sand box
As the days they went by
The smell it got high
And now he's been sent for detox

❄ ❄ ❄

Chapter 6: The Culinary World

A celebrity kitty from Bude
Employed as a tester of food
For a large fee, of course
A brand he'll endorse
He's not only famous but shrewd

❅ ❅ ❅

An Italian cat who ate jelly
Could not understand why his belly
Was so awfully round
That it rolled on the ground
And that's why his name is Pirelli

❄ ❄ ❄

A fat cat who works as a model
Says trying to be thin is just twaddle
I'm the pride of the catwalk
From Milan to New York
Who cares if I walk with a waddle

❋ ❋ ❋

A cat who belonged to a priest
On communion wafers would feast
He'd drink up the wine
Until feeling benign
And bless every bird, mouse and beast

❄ ❄ ❄

Chapter 7: Crime and Punishment

A lawyer who owned a prize bird
Under oath made his cat give his word
But while trying a case
The cat stuffed his face
For to swear before supper's absurd

❊ ❊ ❊

A kitty who stole food for leisure
Would hoard it all just like some treasure
But a fish on a plate
It acted as bait
Now he's awaiting Her Majesty's Pleasure

❋ ❋ ❋

Chapter 8: Show Business

A pedigree Persian from Goring
Thought judges at cat show so boring
But I could be a winner
If only I were thinner
So I'll hold in my tum while they're scoring

A great British cat called Beau
Got bored at a famous cat show
To help pass the time
He did chew on a line
And out all the lights they did go

Chapter 9: Miscellaneous

A foolish young cat from downtown
Would stare at the sky with a frown
He'd wait for a bird
Because he had heard
That what goes up would always come down

❄ ❄ ❄

Old Tom from the Mull of Kintyre
Decided that he would retire
Now the birds and the mice
Think it ever so nice
That he's sitting in front of the fire

❇ ❇ ❇

A cat with great drive and ambition
Did study to be a magician
And he cast a great spell
So that he could foretell
Each mouse and bird's present position

❇ ❇ ❇

Chapter 10: Humphrey

HUMPHREY: WHO LIVED OUT AT KEW
(Who was always polite and so gathered great prosperity)

The nicest cat that ever grew
Was Humphrey who lived out at Kew

He never lost his leather collar
Queens of the night he didn't foller
When eating fish he made no mess
And never clawed his human's dress

He liked, and when within his power
To wash his face upon the hour
And often, at the dinner table
Would beg as far as he was able
To give him if they didn't mind
The chewiest morsels they could find

His later years were just as good
Shown promise of his kitten-hood
In outdoor life he always tried
Avoiding rivals broad and wide

Inside the house he did aspire
To sit politely by the fire
And long before his thirteenth year
Had wedded Gigi

What a gem!
From up the river (Henley-on-Thames)

And there they live in a stately house
Without a hint of rat or mouse
This shows what every cat just might become
By simply being polite

(with apologies to Hilaire Belloc)

❄ ❄ ❄

THE AUTHORS

ulie Hope was born in Sheffield, Yorkshire in 1952. She qualified as a furniture esigner and spent many years in this profession. This not being an occupation with a igh content of fun and flippancy, Julie found a convenient outlet in illustrating, cartoong, and writing whimsical verse. Her cartoons, birthday cards and Christmas cards were ways of enormous delight to family, friends and colleagues. In 1982 Julie emigrated to outh Africa where she later met and married John Hope, an electronics engineer. One ight in 1995 the two of them wrote the songs for Christmas Carols for Cats in the back f a small notebook and on bits of paper serviette whilst dining in a Chinese restaurant in ohannesburg.

hristmas Carols for Cats was published by Bantam in 1996, but to Julie's disappointment e publisher insisted on using their in-house illustrator. Subsequent books, Nursery hymes for Cats, and Christmas Crackers for Cats followed the same format. In 1997 Julie nd John and their four cats relocated to Oxfordshire, UK.

1 2007 John wrote his first full length book, Nine Lives, handsomely illustrated by Julie, hich they self-published in September 2010. Sadly, Julie died later the same month and was John's intention to keep Julie's work alive by continuing to write books and online edia for whimsical cat lovers, using her large archive of unpublished illustrations.

ohn F. Hope was born in Johannesburg, South Africa in 1958 and began writing nthropomorphic stories about animals at age six, encouraged by his grade school teacher. ome of this was frowned upon by the headmaster because said stories failed the test of olitical correctness, even in 1964. John's other passion in life was electronics, which he nthusiastically embraced at age eight and cemented over the next few decades by becomg an electronics engineer of some skill.

1 1990 he met and married Julie, and the whimsical synergy that resulted from this nion led to the publishing of three books by Bantam, Christmas Carols for Cats, Nursery hymes for Cats, and Christmas Crackers for Cats.

ohn passed away suddenly in September 2016, six years after his late wife, Julie - to the ay.

ndrea Hope was born in Baildon, Yorkshire, and studied graphic design. She njoyed a long career in this field, working in advertising, TV and package design before witching to a career in travel in the nineties. John and Andrea met and married in 2011 nd another creative union developed with Andrea producing the covers for her husband's ooks. They lived together with their cats in Longhope, Gloucestershire until John's unmely death.

ndrea has subsequently maintained the cato9tales website, regularly posting John's stute observations, whimsical cat stories and a secret language of cats: Cat Speak. You can ad these wonderful stories here: **www.cato9tales.com**

ndrea has since returned to working full time in photography, and art, producing hand rawn pastel pencil portraits of pets, babies and children.

ee Andrea's work here: **www-pi-artstudios.com**

Copyright

CHRISTMAS CRACKERS FOR CATS

First published in the United Kingdom by Bantam Books Ltd, 2000

Kindle version by Cato9tails Productions 2016

http://www.cato9tales.com

❄ ❄ ❄

OTHER BOOKS BY THE AUTHORS
Christmas Carols for Cats
Nursery Rhymes for Cats
Nine Lives
Hatching Discordia

Printed in Great Britain
by Amazon